P9-CEA-812

For my two great big boys, Robby and Teddy—J.O'C.

To Susan—S.D.S.

G. P. PUTNAM'S SONS
A division of Penguin Young Readers Group. Published by The Penguin Group.
Penguin Group (USA) Inc., 375 Hudson Street, New York, NY 10014, U.S.A.
Penguin Group (Canada), 90 Eglinton Avenue East, Suite 700, Toronto, Ontario, Canada M4P 2Y3 (a division of Pearson Penguin Canada Inc.).
Penguin Books Ltd, 80 Strand, London WC2R 0RL, England.
Penguin Ireland, 25 St. Stephen's Green, Dublin 2, Ireland (a division of Penguin Books Ltd.).
Penguin Group (Australia), 250 Camberwell Road, Camberwell, Victoria 3124, Australia (a division of Pearson Australia Group Pty Ltd).
Penguin Books India Pvt Ltd, 11 Community Centre, Panchsheel Park, New Delhi - 110 017, India.
Penguin Group (NZ), Cnr Airborne and Rosedale Roads, Albany, Auckland 1310, New Zealand (a division of Pearson New Zealand Ltd).
Penguin Books (South Africa) (Pty) Ltd, 24 Sturdee Avenue, Rosebank, Johannesburg 2196, South Africa.
Penguin Books Ltd, Registered Offices: 80 Strand, London WC2R 0RL, England.

Published simultaneously in Canada. Manufactured in China by South China Printing Co. Ltd.
Design by Cecilia Yung and Marikka Tamura. Text set in Biblon.
The pictures were painted with colored inks and gouache.
Library of Congress Cataloging-in-Publication Data
O'Connor, Jane. The snow globe family / by Jane O'Connor ; illustrated by S. D. Schindler. p. cm.
Summary: Two families, one a tiny one that lives in a snow globe in a larger family's home, anxiously await a big snowstorm.
[1. Snowdomes—Fiction. 2. Snow—Fiction. 3. Family—Fiction.] I. Schindler, S. D., ill. II. Title. PZ7.O222Sno 2006 [E]—dc22 2005028560
ISBN 0-399-24242-2
3 5 7 9 10 8 6 4 2

THE SNOW GLOBE FAMILY

By JANE O'CONNOR • Illustrated by S. D. SCHINDLER

G. P. PUTNAM'S SONS

In a big house high on a hill lives a family—
a mama, a papa, a boy, a girl, and Baby.

On the mantel in the parlor sits a snow globe.
It has been there such a long time, nobody notices
it anymore—nobody except Baby.

"Who would like more tea or crumb cake?"
the mama asks.

Inside the snow globe lives another family.
A very little family—a mama, a papa, a boy, a girl,
and a little baby.

They are having dessert too, only their cups are so small,
each one holds no more than half a drop of tea.
　　"Who would like another crumb of crumb cake?"
the little mama asks.

In the snow globe, sparkly snow
covers the ground all year round.
The little family doesn't mind.
They love snow.

They build snowmen as big as
lumps of sugar.

They skate on a pond
as shiny as a silver coin.

They throw snowballs, make snow angels, and tramp
through the snow, leaving footprints smaller than the sprinkles
on an ice cream cone.

If only someone in the big family would shake the snow globe
really hard and make a hill of snow. Then the little family could
go sledding.

Sometimes the little family shouts, "Hellooooo, out there! Look at us!"
But the big papa is reading aloud a story. Nobody notices them—
nobody except Baby.

The little papa is reading a story too. When he's done, the children
say, "Tell us about the big snowstorms from long ago. Pleeeease, Papa."
"There used to be snowstorms all the time. Big ones!" their
papa begins.

"The house rattled and shook. Dishes flew from the cupboards, furniture slid across the floor.

Once I got thrown out of the bathtub! Those were the days."

Now there's only a gentle
flurry once a week when the
parlor maid dusts the mantel.

Inside the snow globe, nobody except
the little baby notices. A flurry—who cares?
What the family wants is a great big snowstorm. A blizzard!

That's what the children in the big house are hoping for too. A blizzard. And one evening, snow starts to fall and doesn't stop.

It is a perfect night for sledding. Off they go, leaving Baby behind.

"It is your bedtime. The snow will still be here tomorrow," the mama says and goes upstairs to run Baby's bath.

But Baby wants snow now!

Baby pushes her papa's footstool over to the mantel. She piles books and pillows on top. Then up she climbs.

Who does she see inside the snow globe?

She sees the little baby!
What does the little baby see—
two enormous eyes!

Baby grabs the snow globe. Oops! The books and pillows slip from under her. She lands on the pillows and giggles.

She shakes the snow globe. She shakes it some more.

Inside the snow globe, the little family hangs on for dear life.

"Th-th-th-this is s-s-s-some st-storm!"

In the big house, Baby hears her mama calling. "Come, Baby. We'll go sledding too. The snow is too wonderful to miss."

Inside the snow globe, the little family runs outside.
There is a perfect hill for sledding.

It is late now. In the big house,
the mama, the papa, and the children
are upstairs, fast asleep.

The snow globe is up on the mantel again.
The little family is fast asleep too.

Everyone—big and little—is dreaming about the next big snowstorm.

Who knows?
It might come very soon.